To:

_____

From:

_____

Date:

_____

I PRAYED FOR YOU

Jean Fischer

Illustrated by
Frank Endersby

Tommy
NELSON®

An Imprint of Thomas Nelson

For all the mamas who prayed for their babies
and for the mamas-at-heart still waiting.

I Prayed for You

© 2015, 2018 by Thomas Nelson

Illustrated by Frank Endersby

Published in Nashville, Tennessee, by Tommy Nelson. Tommy Nelson is an imprint of Thomas Nelson. Thomas Nelson is a registered trademark of HarperCollins Christian Publishing, Inc.

Tommy Nelson titles may be purchased in bulk for educational, business, fund-raising, or sales promotional use. For information, please e-mail SpecialMarkets@ThomasNelson.com.

Scripture quotations are taken from the *Holy Bible*, New Living Translation. © 1996, 2004, 2007, 2013 by Tyndale House Foundation. Used by permission of Tyndale House Publishers, Inc., Carol Stream, Illinois 60188. All rights reserved.

ISBN-13: 978-1-4003-1281-8

Library of Congress Cataloging-in-Publication Data

Names: Fischer, Jean, author. | Endersby, Frank, illustrator.
Title: I prayed for you / by Jean Fischer ; illustrated by Frank Endersby
Description: Nashville, Tennessee : Thomas Nelson, [2018]
Identifiers: LCCN 2017031047 | ISBN 9781400312818 (hardback)
Subjects: LCSH: Children--Prayers and devotions. | Bears--Miscellanea.
Classification: LCC BL625.5 .F57 2018 | DDC 242/.62--dc23 LC record available at
https://lccn.loc.gov/2017031047

Printed in China

18 19 20 21 22 DSC 6 5 4 3 2 1

Mfr: DSC / Shenzhen, China / February 2018 / PO #9465689

Children are a gift from the LORD.

—Psalm 127:3

Before you were born, I asked God for something special. I asked Him for you.

"Dear loving Father in heaven above, send a sweet baby for Mama to love."

The first time I held you in my arms,
you fell asleep all snuggly-cozy.
And I prayed.

"Thank You, dear God, for this cute, cuddly bear.
May my little one know Your love's always there."

When you took your first wobbly, little steps,
I asked God to guide you wherever you go.

"Guide every step—every day, every year.
Help this cub follow You and to You draw near."

The first time you made a big tower with blocks, you needed some help to reach the top. I smiled as I prayed.

"Watch over my little one all the day long,
and help my bear cub grow up big and strong."

One day I gave you colorful paints and brushes,
and you painted your first picture.
As I hung it on the wall, I prayed.

"Thank You, dear God, for my bear cub's sweet heart.
To me, this child is Your great work of art."

When you said your first prayers,
your voice was like a song—the sweetest song
I have ever heard. And God heard you too.

"Listen, dear Lord, as my munchkin prays.
May this heart turn to You and love You always."

You said your first no when you should have said yes.
But Mama never, ever stopped loving you.
I asked God for help.

"Please help my child to learn what is good
and to do what a dear little honey bear should."

The first time you saw a butterfly, it fluttered
around your fuzzy head, and it tickled your little,
round ears. You laughed, and I prayed.

"God, give this silly bear dances and wiggles,
the happiest fun, and bundles of giggles!"

The first time you got hurt, I gave you the biggest, warmest, safest mama hug, and I asked God to make you all better again.

"Whenever my sweetie pie hurts for a while,
please change that sad face from a frown to a smile."

On that day when you first put your clothes on all by yourself, I was so proud of you! We sang and we danced. And I said, "Thank You, God."

"Thank You so much for each little blessing.
Today we are grateful for by-myself dressing!"

Your first fishing trip was full of adventure.
You didn't give up when that fish was so big!
And I prayed for us.

"In everything we do, in work and in play,
help us honor You each and every day."

Then, one day, you were so brave.
You spent the whole day at school without me.
And while you were gone, I asked God to help you.

"My little one's headed for classrooms and hallways.
Please go with my pumpkin today and then always."

At your first game, you put on your jersey and played your very hardest. And then you made your first friend, and I was so grateful.

"Thank You, dear Lord, for my little one's friend.
Playmates are one of the best gifts You send!"

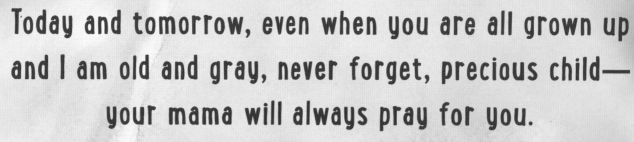

Today and tomorrow, even when you are all grown up and I am old and gray, never forget, precious child— your mama will always pray for you.

"Dear loving Father in heaven above,
thank You so much for this child I love. Amen."